Croft

Comic-Strip Writing Prompts

by Karen Kellaher

SCHOLASTIC
PROFESSIONAL BOOKS

New York ★ Toronto ★ London ★ Auckland ★ Sydney

Mexico City ★ New Delhi ★ Hong Kong

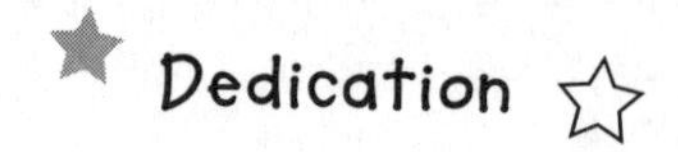

Dedication

With love to my grandmother, Anna Gertrude Burns

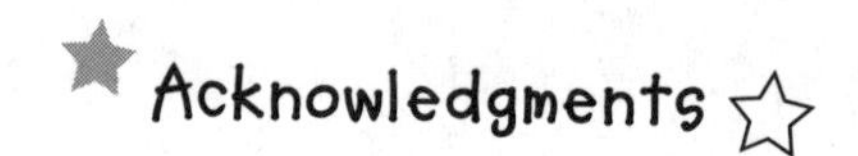

Acknowledgments

The publisher thanks the following copyright holders for permission to use the strips in this book: Universal Press Syndicate, United Media, North America Syndicate, and King Features Syndicate.

Cover design by Pamela Simmons
Cover illustration by Norma Ortiz
Interior design by Grafica, Inc.
ISBN: 0-439-15977-6

CONTENTS

My fondness for newspaper comic strips dates back several decades to my own elementary school days. Although I am trained as a journalist and have spent much of my adult life as a consumer, writer, and editor of news, I admit that it was the ink-laden funny pages that first attracted me to the daily newspaper that graced my family's coffee table. Back then, comics were such a prevalent part of kid culture! I still remember that my third-grade reading group proudly—and unanimously—dubbed itself "Peanuts" after Charles Schulz's beloved strip.

Today a lot has changed. Many people get their daily dose of news from television or an Internet service rather than a print newspaper. But as far as I can tell, kids still love comics—and these witty strips continue to influence our popular culture. Step into any toy store or T-shirt shop and you'll see an amazing variety of merchandise sporting popular comic-strip characters. Even my preschooler recognizes Garfield and Snoopy. And I have noticed that when today's media-savvy children pick up a newspaper, they *still* turn to the comic section first. For educators, the message is clear: By using comic strips in your classroom, you can tap into students' enthusiasm and turn the writing process into an enjoyable, laughing matter. This book, the latest in Scholastic's popular line of writing-prompt collections, is a great place to start!

An All-American Art Form

By using comics in your classroom, you are celebrating an art form that is uniquely American. The first real newspaper comics appeared in this country in the late nineteenth century, as big-city newspapers competed fiercely for readers. The competition was especially tough in New York City, where newspaper publishers Joseph Pulitzer and William Randolph Hearst waged an all-out war. The rival publishers learned that readers were drawn to illustrations, and in the mid 1890s Pulitzer unleashed a new weapon in the battle for readers. It was a simple but funny Sunday strip called *The Doings in Hogan's Alley* (later renamed *The Yellow Kid*) by Richard Felton Outcault. The new feature was unlike anything newspaper readers had seen before: It was a sequence of pictures supplemented by limited text and dialogue, and it featured a cast of characters readers could come to know and love. The strip was wildly popular, and soon both newspapers were boasting comic strips as a selling point.

Today there are hundreds of newspaper comic strips, some told in single panels, others in a series of frames. Some strips are simply humorous, while others are satirical or reflective. These newspaper "funnies" often make telling statements about the world in which we live; they help us see the comedy and drama in our own lives.

Finding Inspiration in the Funny Pages

Using comic strips to inspire young writers makes sense for many reasons. First, comics can ease one of the toughest parts of the writing process: finding ideas and getting started. As you know, many students regularly groan that they "don't have anything to write about." But introducing and discussing a comic strip can help get their creative juices flowing. Because students come to know comic characters well, they feel as if old friends are guiding them into the writing process. Because the comics touch on a variety of kid-friendly, compelling issues, students won't have any problem coming up with ideas to write about! And best of all, because this book includes so many comics on so many topics, you'll be able to make writing a regular part of every day, an important step in nurturing children into literacy.

A second reason it makes sense to use comics to teach writing is that they appeal to readers of all levels. The pictures and simple text work together to help struggling readers successfully read a strip. At the same time, students won't feel as though the material is babyish; most kids are proud to read newspaper comic strips because they see the strips as something grown-ups enjoy.

A third—and very important—reason to teach writing with comic strips is that comics often call upon students' higher-order thinking skills. A comic rarely states its main idea outright; instead it implies or gently hints at its message. That means your students will put their thinking skills to the test as they interpret, reflect, and write.

Special Features of This Book

This prompt collection is designed to meet the needs of busy teachers who want to make writing enjoyable, relaxing, and meaningful. In this book, you will find the following:

- creative prompts that help students practice a wide variety of writing genres and call upon young writers to predict outcomes, understand the main idea, compare and contrast, make character sketches, generate lists, connect the comics to their own lives, express their own opinions, and more
- background information about the featured comic strips, characters, and cartoonists
- a thematic banner at the top of each page for easy reference
- a topical index (page 64) to help you find prompts that connect to your curriculum
- two or more prompts for each comic strip so you can choose which is best for your class or allow students to choose their favorite prompt
- a resource list (page 63) including Web sites and books to help you create additional comic-strip writing prompts

Using the Prompts

The following tips will help you make the most of the comic-strip prompts:

1. Read aloud or make copies of the background information and character sketches provided for each comic strip. This will help your students become more familiar with the strip—and better able to respond creatively to the writing prompts.

2. Allow your students to choose the prompt they'd like to respond to for each strip (each strip includes two thought-provoking prompts). Each prompt includes several questions or ideas for writing topics. Children can choose from among these prompts based on the direction in which they wish to take their writing. They don't need to answer every question.

3. Use the Web addresses and other resources listed in the back of the book to e-mail or write to a cartoonist whose work your class particularly admires. Students can pose questions and express their admiration while building letter-writing skills.

4. In addition to having students respond in writing to each comic strip, invite them to act out the scenes. Students can use their imagination to portray what happened before the first illustrated frame—or what might happen next.

5. As you read the daily newspaper, keep your eyes open for comic strips that relate to your curriculum. Clip them out and write your own prompts to go with each one. Encourage students to do the same.

6. Use the prompts as part of a classroom Comic Corner. Make copies of some of the prompts, and store them in a folder or binder in a designated area of your classroom. Send students to the Comic Corner when they finish work early, while you are working with small groups, or when individual students are looking for something to do.

GARFIELD

Created by Jim Davis

Background Information

Garfield is among the best known and most beloved comic characters ever created. When this humorous strip about a lazy tabby cat was first syndicated in 1978, it appeared in 41 newspapers. Today it is printed in more than 2,600 newspapers around the world. The comic strip is the most widely syndicated Sunday strip in the United States, and it has more than 220 million faithful readers. Collections of *Garfield* strips have been translated into 26 languages and have frequently hit the tops of best-seller lists. Through the years, the comic strip has given rise to a popular animated CBS television series, *Garfield and Friends*, and more than a dozen prime-time TV specials.

Garfield cartoonist Jim Davis began drawing when he was a child. As a result of his asthma, Davis spent much of his free time indoors with pencils and paper. And his family's farm provided plenty of inspiration for drawing cartoon cats: At one time more than two dozen cats roamed the property! Today Davis has a dog named Molly, but, surprisingly, he does not own a cat.

Because *Garfield* has an audience that spans many nations and generations, it usually deals with simple, universal themes such as friendship, as well as daily routines such as sleeping, eating, and watching television. With his wit and subtle wisdom, Garfield the cat is sure to delight your young readers!

Cast of Characters

Garfield: A lazy tabby cat who loves naps and every kind of food except vegetables

Jon Arbuckle: Garfield's kind owner, who leads a simple life and always seems to be serving Garfield a meal

Odie: The other pet in the Arbuckle household. Often teased by Garfield, Odie is not the smartest dog under the sun!

Pooky: Garfield's beloved teddy bear

Name ______________________________ Date ____________

Number One Pet?

Write About It: Which animal makes a better pet: a dog or a cat? Write an imaginary debate on this topic between Garfield the cat and Odie the dog. Have each animal argue why he deserves the title "the country's favorite pet."

Keep Going: On a piece of posterboard, draw a picture of your favorite pet. It can be a real pet that you know or one you'd like to have one day. Beneath the picture, write at least five sentences explaining why this pet is so great. Be sure to give your poster a title, too!

Name ______________________ Date ____________

Dream On

Write About It: What did Garfield do while he was dreaming? How do you suppose Jon, his owner, will react? Do you think cats and other animals really dream? If so, what do you think they dream about? Choose three kinds of animals and describe a dream each one might have.

____

____

____

____

____

____

____

____

____

____

Keep Going: What is the strangest dream you remember having? Write a story telling what happened in your dream. Include as many details as you can, such as the setting or location of your dream, the characters in your dream, and even how you felt.

Name ____________________ Date ____________

Rise and Shine

Write About It: Do you think Garfield is a morning "person"? Are you a morning person, an afternoon person, or a night owl? Tell which time of day you like the best—and which time you like the least. Based on this information, would you and Garfield make good housemates?

Keep Going: Do you agree with Jon that breakfast is the most important meal of the day? What do you usually eat for breakfast? What is your favorite breakfast food? Do you ever skip the morning meal? If so, how do you feel during the day?

Name ______________________ Date ____________

Chore Time

Write About It: What does Garfield mean when he says, "Now I'm a procrastinator"? Use clues from the comic strip to define this word, or look it up in a dictionary. Have you ever been a procrastinator? Describe a time when you waited until the last minute to do something.

Keep Going: If you could give your pet a list of chores, what three tasks would you have the pet do? Why? Before you answer, think about the animal's special talents or habits. What kind of reward would you give your pet in return for finishing the chores? (If you don't have a pet, you can make a list of chores for a pet you would like to have.)

Name ______________________ Date ____________

TV Trouble

Write About It: Based on this comic strip, do you think Garfield is a frequent television viewer? What clues in the strip helped you answer? What do *you* think: Can television damage a person's intelligence? Explain your ideas and give examples whenever possible.

____

____

____

____

____

____

____

____

____

____

Keep Going: How many hours of TV do you watch each week? How else could you spend that time? Make a list of ten activities you could do instead of watching TV. Be sure to include things you can do by yourself, things you can do with friends, and things you can do with family members.

Name ______________________ Date ____________

Monday Blues

Write About It: What makes Garfield realize that it is Monday? Based on this strip, how do you think he feels about Mondays? How do *you* feel about Mondays? Explain why you either like or dislike them.

Keep Going: List the seven days of the week. Write one reason why you like each day. Is there something you look forward to doing on particular days? Which day of the week is your favorite and why?

Name ______________________ Date __________

Remote Control

Write About It: Is Garfield interested in learning more about the inventor of the remote control? How do you know? Do you think Garfield likes the remote control? Why or why not? List *your* five favorite inventions of all time. Why is each one important or useful to you?

Keep Going: Like most inventions, the television remote control was created to make people's lives easier. Think of your own invention to make your life easier. Tell how it would work, what you would call it, and when you would use it.

Name ______________________________ Date ______________

Cat Got Your Tongue?

Write About It: Do you agree with Garfield's comment that if cats could talk, nobody would like them? Why or why not? What *would* cats say if they could speak? How would talking cats compare with other creatures? If all animals could speak, which do you think would be the funniest? The friendliest? The grouchiest?

____

____

____

____

____

____

____

____

____

____

____

Keep Going: Write a short story in which a talking animal is the main character. You may feature Garfield as the animal or create a character of your own.

Name ______________________ Date ____________

The Worst Day

Write About It: Tell what you think has happened to Jon in the last frame of the comic strip. Has he been whisked away by aliens from outer space? Has he landed in the cat box in the basement? Use your imagination! Then compare Jon's "bad day" with Garfield's. What kinds of disasters might have happened to each character throughout the day? In your opinion, whose day was worse?

Keep Going: What makes you feel better after you've had a bad day? Do you like to relax with a good book? Go for a long bike ride? What activities would you recommend to someone who has had a terrible day?

Name ____________________ Date __________

Tall Tales

Write About It: Why do you think Garfield is telling Jon about mutant spiders and giant tidal waves? Can you tell if he is trying to trick Jon? Does his trick work? How does Jon react to Garfield in each frame of the comic strip?

Keep Going: What if one of Garfield's wild stories were really true? Write a newspaper story about mutant spiders crushing the city, a tidal wave striking, or some other incredible event. Be sure to answer the questions *who, what, when, where, why,* and *how*. Give your news story a headline and draw a picture to go with it.

Name ______________________________ Date ______________

Something's Fishy

Write About It: How do you think Garfield feels about fishing? Explain. What kind of sport is just right for *you*? A relaxing fishing trip? A fast-paced game of ice hockey? Do you prefer team sports or sports you play alone? Why?

____

____

____

____

____

____

____

____

____

____

____

Keep Going: Add some excitement to Garfield's day of fishing! What kind of adventure could he and Jon have on the lake? Describe the adventure and draw some pictures to illustrate the action. In the end, would Garfield still feel the same way about fishing?

Name ______________________ Date ______________

Cat-sup Caper

Write About It: What is Garfield doing in this comic strip? Is he really trying to help Jon by putting catsup on the eggs—or is he up to no good? Why do you think so? If you were Jon, what would you do next?

___

___

___

___

___

___

___

___

___

___

___

Keep Going: As the comic strip shows, a food that is delicious to one person may not be so appetizing to another. Describe one of your favorite snacks or meals that others might not like. When did you first try this food? What could you say to others to convince them to try it? Share your answer with your class.

Name ______________________________ Date ______________

Pets at Play

Write About It: Do you think Garfield is bored? Do you think real pets get bored when they are home alone? Explain your answer. Think about how your pet or a friend's pet spends the day. Describe a game or pastime the pet might enjoy when no one else is around.

____

____

____

____

____

____

____

____

____

____

____

Keep Going: Do you enjoy being by yourself sometimes? Why or why not? What games or activities do you like to do when you are by yourself?

Name ______________________ Date ____________

Wild Weather

Write About It: Have you ever experienced a terrible snowstorm, hurricane, or other wild weather event like the one in the comic strip? Describe your experience. What did it look like outside? What sounds did you hear? How did you stay safe, and how did you feel? (If you have never experienced stormy weather, imagine and describe what a storm might be like.)

____

____

____

____

____

____

____

____

____

____

Keep Going: What type of weather do you suppose Garfield likes best? Why? What is your favorite type of weather? What is your least favorite? Explain your responses.

Name ______________________________ Date ______________

Creepy Crawlers

Write About It: What makes this strip funny is that the reader knows something that Garfield does not know. What is it? What do you think will happen next in the strip? Write a paragraph describing your prediction, and draw a picture to go with it.

____

____

____

____

____

____

____

____

____

____

Keep Going: How do you think Garfield feels about spiders? Do you feel that way about anything? Explain. Then make a poster to help people with arachnophobia (fear of spiders). Find some reassuring facts about spiders in books or on the Internet. For example, do they usually hurt people? Where do they live? Include these facts as well as a drawing of a spider.

Name ______________________ Date ______________

No More Veggies

Write About It: Why do you think Jon is trying to get Garfield to eat vegetables? How do you suppose Garfield feels about veggies? Invent a fun new way for junk-food lovers like Garfield to eat their vegetables. For example, you might invent a spinach donut or a veggie milkshake. Be sure to list the ingredients and give your invention a neat name!

____

____

____

____

____

____

____

____

____

____

Keep Going: Which vegetables do like best? Which do you like least? Jot down the names of ten veggies and rank them from 1 to 10, with 1 being the best. Write a few sentences explaining why you chose the veggies at the top and bottom of your list.

PEANUTS

Created by Charles M. Schulz

Background Information

Peanuts, which first appeared in a handful of American newspapers in 1950, had one of the largest and most devoted followings of any comic strip. At the time of Charles Schulz's retirement in late 1999, the strip appeared in more than 2,000 newspapers in 68 countries and was translated into 26 languages. Charles Schulz passed away on February 12, 2000 at the age of 77.

The lovable *Peanuts* gang has starred in four movies, several television specials, a Broadway musical, and a variety of other media. The strip has also won countless awards. Your students may find it interesting that the strip originally was called *L'il Folks*—and was rejected six times before being accepted by United Feature Syndicate.

Although the *Peanuts* readership spanned all ages, the strip is credited with being one of the first newspaper comics to address children's real fears, frustrations, and hopes. Typical topics included the pressures of playing sports, challenges at school, and other day-to-day issues that kids face.

Cast of Characters

Charlie Brown: Nicknamed "Blockhead" by his friends, Charlie often worries and thinks about the true meaning of life.

Snoopy: Charlie Brown's pet beagle, who dreams of all kinds of exciting adventures. Snoopy does not speak, but he communicates through comic thought bubbles and facial expressions.

Lucy Van Pelt: In control and occasionally grouchy, Lucy craves compliments and attention.

Linus Van Pelt: Lucy's brother, who totes around a security blanket and comes up with wise solutions to all kinds of problems

Schroeder: One of the quietest members of the Peanuts gang, Schroeder spends all his time playing his piano and ignoring Lucy's flirtations.

Sally Brown: Charlie Brown's little sister, who is always searching for the easy way out—especially when it comes to schoolwork

Peppermint Patty: A fun-loving character who loves baseball, Patty is a good friend to Charlie Brown, whom she calls "Chuck."

Woodstock: A tiny bird, who is Snoopy's closest friend and playmate

Name ______________________________ Date ______________

Excuses, Excuses!

PEANUTS reprinted by permission of United Feature Syndicate, Inc.

Write About It: Create a "Top 10" list of funny excuses Lucy could have given Charlie Brown for missing the ball (in addition to the excuse she gave in the strip). Was she distracted by an alien spaceship? Frozen in place by a magician's spell? Use your imagination! When you are done, come up with some funny excuses for an embarrassing moment of your own.

____

____

____

____

____

____

____

____

____

____

Keep Going: How do you think Lucy feels in the first part of this comic? Have *you* ever missed the ball during an important game? Tripped in the middle of a dance recital? Tell about an embarrassing moment you have experienced. Explain how you felt during and after the blooper. Then draw a picture to show what happened.

Name ______________________ Date ____________

Good-bye, Summer

Write About It: How does Sally feel about the end of summer? Did you ever feel that way? Sally's teacher has asked her to write about what she did last summer. You have probably written about this same topic many times! Now write about a summer that you would *like* to experience! Pretend you are enjoying the summer of your dreams. Write a letter to a friend telling him or her all about your imaginary summer adventures.

____

____

____

____

____

____

____

____

____

____

Keep Going: In some places (maybe even where you live), kids go to school year-round, with short vacations throughout the year. Do you think Sally would enjoy such a setup? Would you? Make a chart listing the pros and cons of a year-round school schedule.

Name ______________________________ Date ______________

Kids Are People, Too!

Write About It: How do you think Linus feels in this comic strip? Do you agree that no one asks kids for their opinions? What are some opinions you have that you would like to express to others? Explain your opinions and give reasons why you feel the way you do.

____

____

____

____

____

____

____

____

____

____

Keep Going: Write a letter to the editor of your local newspaper on a topic that is important to you. Clearly state your opinion, and give some facts to support it. Then proofread and send your letter to the newspaper! (Check the editorial pages for the address.)

Name ______________________________ Date ______________

Animal Helpers

PEANUTS reprinted by permission of United Feature Syndicate, Inc.

Write About It: What is the topic of Sally's school report? Help Sally finish her report by answering the following questions: What are some ways in which animals help humans? Do you think people treat animals fairly? Why or why not?

____

____

____

____

____

____

____

____

____

____

____

Keep Going: Do you think animals should have rights? If so, imagine that you are a lawmaker and it is your job to come up with an Animal Bill of Rights for all animals in general or for your favorite species. List each right and tell why each is important. If you don't think animals should have rights, explain why.

Name ____________________ Date ____________

Be a Good Sport

Write About It: In your opinion, what does it mean to be a "good sport"? Do you think Lucy is being a good sport in this comic strip? Why or why not? What are some ways that athletes can be good sports? Do you think it is hard to be a good sport when you lose a game or contest? Explain.

____

____

____

____

____

____

____

____

____

____

____

Keep Going: Imagine that you are the coach of a sports team and that your team just lost a big game. How do you think your team members feel? What could you say to help them feel better? Write a short speech you would give to your team after the game.

DENNIS THE MENACE

Created by Hank Ketcham

Background Information

Comic-strip readers have enjoyed the mischief of *Dennis the Menace* for more than half a century. The strip first appeared in American newspapers in 1950, and it is now syndicated in more than 1,200 papers in 48 countries. Over the years, this popular strip has been the subject of a television series, two hit movies, countless books, and thousands of licensed products. The strip's star character, young Dennis Mitchell, has been used in public-relations campaigns for the Boy Scouts of America, UNICEF, and other prominent organizations.

Creator Hank Ketcham produced the daily and Sunday *Dennis the Menace* strips himself until 1994, when he turned the reins over to two assistant artists, Marcus Hamilton and Ronald Ferdinand. Ketcham, now in his eighties, continues to supervise work on the strip.

Cast of Characters

Dennis Mitchell: An active, curious boy who has been "five an' a half" years old since the strip was created in 1950. Dennis's mischief is always getting him into trouble with his parents and with his neighbor Mr. Wilson.

Alice Mitchell: Dennis's mother, who seems to have a never-ending supply of patience and love

Henry Mitchell: Dennis's father, an aeronautical engineer

George Wilson: The Mitchells' grouchy next-door neighbor, whom Dennis visits frequently and badgers with a million questions

Martha Wilson: George's kind wife, who opens her heart and kitchen to little Dennis

Joey: Dennis's best friend

Margaret: A girl who lives in the neighborhood

Ruff: Dennis's pet dog

Name ______________________________ Date ______________

In the Doghouse

Write About It: What do you think Dennis has done to make his mom angry? Make up a story to explain why Dennis is in trouble, and set it up in comic-strip form.

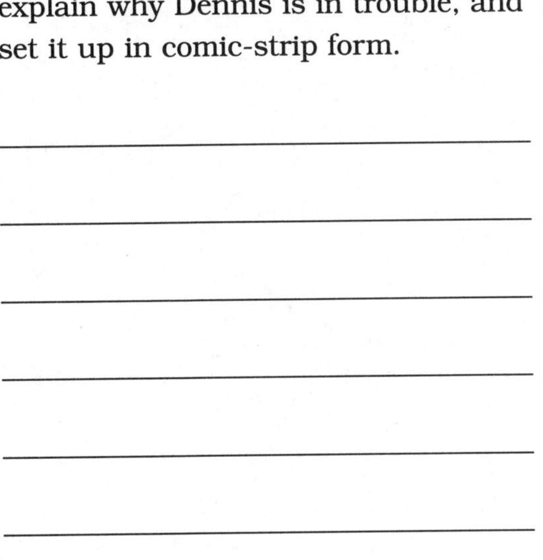

"MOVE OVER, BOY. I'M GONNA STAY WITH YOU 'TIL MOM COOLS OFF."

Keep Going: What does it mean when we say someone is "in the doghouse"? Where do you suppose this expression came from? Have you ever felt as though you were in the doghouse? How did it feel?

Name ______________________ Date ____________

Storm Stories

Write About It: Almost everyone has a story to explain why thunder happens. What is Dennis's explanation? Can you make up your own folktale to explain thunder and lightning? (Remember that a folktale is a story people create, often to explain something in nature. It is not really true.)

"DON'T WORRY ABOUT *THUNDER*, JOEY. IT'S JUST THE CLOUDS **SNORING!**"

____

____

____

____

____

____

____

____

____

____

____

____

____

____

Keep Going: Do thunderstorms send you running scared—or do you enjoy thunder and lightning? Explain.

Name ______________________ Date ____________

Camping Out

Write About It: What have Dennis and Joey brought along on their "camping" trip? Why is this funny? Do you think you would like camping? Why or why not? How long could you live without conveniences such as TV, refrigerators, or comfortable beds? What would you miss most while camping?

www.kingfeatures.com
Ketcham
7-7
© 1998, North America Synd.
"WE'LL HAFTA CAMP HERE, JOEY. THIS IS AS FAR AS THE 'LECTRIC CORD WILL STRETCH."

____

____

____

____

____

____

____

____

____

____

____

____

____

Keep Going: Like many of the things in your home, Dennis's television needs electricity to run. Make a list of all the electrical gadgets and appliances your family uses in one day. Then imagine what you would do if the electricity failed for a whole day. How would you spend your time? How would you cook meals?

Name ______________________ Date ____________

Grandparent Appreciation

Write About It: Based on this strip, how would you describe Dennis's relationship with his grandfather? Are you close to a grandparent or other special relative? Tell why you think the person is special, and describe an activity you enjoy doing together.

"I LIKE WALKIN' WITH GRAMPA. HE'S JUST MY SPEED."

____

____

____

____

____

____

____

____

____

____

____

____

____

____

Keep Going: Many older people do not have grandchildren to spend time with. You can brighten the day of an older neighbor or nursing home resident by writing and illustrating a funny story for him or her to enjoy. Or make your own mini-book full of jokes and riddles.

Name ____________________ Date __________

Stargazing

Write About It: What does Mr. Wilson mean by "counting your lucky stars"? What does Dennis think he means? Think about your own life. What are your lucky stars? Make a list of the things you are most thankful for, and write a sentence or two about each one.

"MR. WILSON SAYS I SHOULD COUNT MY LUCKY STARS...BUT I DON'T KNOW WHICH ONES ARE MINE."

Keep Going: Imagine that you could own a star or planet. What would you name yours? Why? What would daily life be like in this place?

Name ______________________ Date ____________

Toy Trouble

Write About It: Why might Dennis's neighbor Mr. Wilson be hiding the boys' football? Make up a funny story to explain why. Then describe what Dennis and Joey could do to get their ball back.

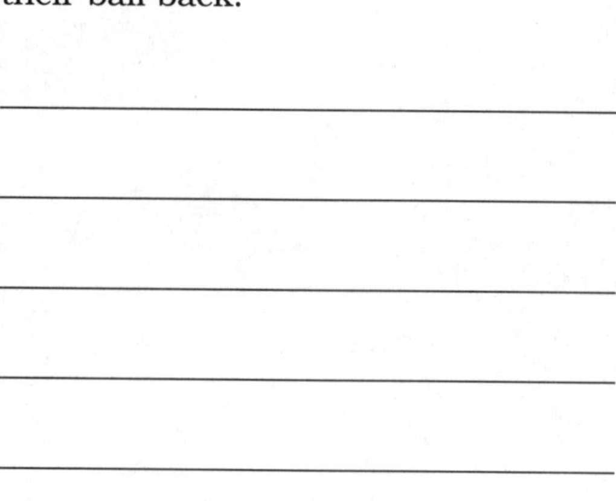

"MIND IF WE PLAY WITH YOUR DOLL? MR.WILSON'S HIDING OUR FOOTBALL!"

Keep Going: What are some of your favorite toys? Explain what you like best about each. If you could invent a toy, what would it be? What would you call it?

Name ______________________ Date ____________

Time for a Raise?

Write About It: What does Dennis's dad mean? Does Dennis's dad really get an allowance? Explain. Is Dennis's dad being fair? Do you think kids should get allowances? If so, how much? Should kids do chores to earn the money?

"DAD SAYS I CAN'T GET A RAISE IN *MY* ALLOWANCE UNTIL HE GETS A RAISE IN HIS."

Keep Going: What kinds of things do you imagine Dennis and Joey need money for? How could they earn it (besides asking for more allowance)? Write a story in which the boys try to raise money for a special item. What money-raising scheme do they come up with? Is it a success or a big flop?

Name ______________________________ Date ______________

Mailbox Blues

Write About It: What do you think Dennis and Mr. Wilson mean by "junk mail"? Why does Mr. Wilson complain about this kind of mail? Why do you think businesses send so much junk mail to people? What is your favorite kind of mail? If you could receive a letter from anyone, who would it be?

"MR. WILSON GETS SO MUCH JUNK MAIL, HE CALLS HIS LETTER BOX A *LITTER* BOX."

Keep Going: For several days, keep track of the junk mail your family receives. Or ask your principal or school secretary to pass along the junk mail delivered to your school. Write a letter to one of the junk-mail companies asking it to take your family or school off its mailing list. Or make a list of the ways you could use junk mail to keep it from getting thrown into the garbage.

Name ______________________________ Date ______________

What's News?

Write About It: Do you agree with Dennis that television news can be frightening? Which do you think is more frightening: a scary movie or the news? Explain. In your opinion, should kids be allowed to watch scary things on TV and in the movies? If so, at what age?

"MY MOM WON'T LET ME SEE SCARY MOVIES, SO I WATCH THE NEWS INSTEAD."

____

____

____

____

____

____

____

____

____

____

____

____

____

Keep Going: It's time for some good news! Talk to students, teachers, and other people in your school community to learn about some of the wonderful things going on. Is your school planning to build a playground? Has a student won a special award? Use your school's good news to write an imaginary television news broadcast. You and your classmates can "produce" the broadcast for the rest of the school.

Name ______________________ Date ____________

Birds on the Go

Write About It: What are the ducks doing in this comic strip? If you could choose a place to spend the winter months, where would it be? Why? Create a travel brochure advertising your special place. Be sure to describe the weather and some fun activities you might do there.

"TOO BAD YOU'RE NOT A DUCK, MARGARET. THINK OF ALL THE KEEN PLACES YOU COULD SPEND THE WINTER!"

Keep Going: In some parts of the country, seeing birds migrate south is a sign that winter is approaching—and seeing the birds return months later is a sign of spring. What are the signs of winter where you live? What are the signs of spring?

Name ______________________ Date ____________

Mall Madness

"IT'S TOO NICE OF A DAY TO STAY INSIDE. LET'S GO TO THE MALL!"

Write About It: What do you think of Dennis's comment in the comic strip? Do you like going to a shopping mall? Why or why not? Make a list of ten things Dennis could do in addition to or instead of going to the mall.

Keep Going: Some people like to shop, but others can't stand it! If you were building a mall, what would you do to make it a pleasant experience for everyone? Draw a picture showing some of the special features you would include for people who don't enjoy shopping. Would you have comfy lounge chairs? A playground? Use your imagination!

Name ______________________ Date ____________

The Best Medicine

Write About It: How do you think Dennis feels in this comic strip? How can you tell? What do you think of Dennis's idea for a cold medicine that tastes like ketchup? If you could design a medicine that kids would not mind taking, what would it taste like?

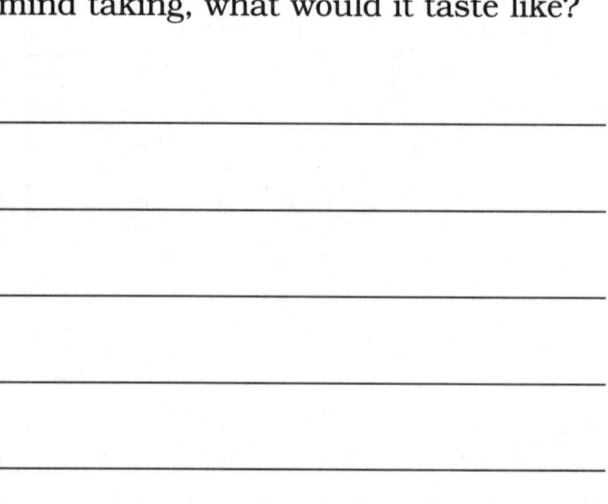

"YUK! WHEN ARE THEY GONNA INVENT A COUGH SYRUP THAT TASTES LIKE KETCHUP?"

Keep Going: In your opinion, what's the worst part of being sick with a cold or the flu? What—or who—makes you feel better when you are sick? Why?

CLAIRE AND WEBER

Created by Doug Shannon

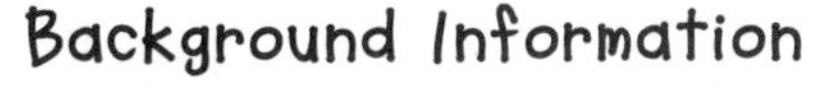

Background Information

Claire and Weber, created by Doug Shannon, is a daily comic strip about a girl's adventures at school and at home. Claire is an ambitious eight-year-old who dramatizes the events of everyday life in an appealing and humorous way. Weber the frog is one of Claire's friends. (Weber does not appear in the strips in this book, but he is often featured in the regular strip.) *Claire and Weber* was launched in 1998 and is syndicated by King Features Syndicate to approximately 25 newspapers.

As a boy, Doug Shannon loved delivering the morning newspaper—and his favorite part was getting to read the funny pages. He especially admired the comic strips by cartoonists Al Capp and Charles Schultz. Before switching gears in his forties to become a cartoonist, Shannon worked as a successful animator, illustrator, and caricaturist.

Shannon says he hopes the strip *Claire and Weber* promotes laughter and self-reflection in both children and adults. The heroine's typical exploits involve friendships, crushes, secrets, name-calling, and more—all real-life issues that resonate with readers of all ages.

Cast of Characters

Claire: A smart elementary school student who worries about popularity, grades, and more

Amy: Claire's bright friend, who is a perfectionist

Jason Grimes: The school bully

Raina: The most popular girl at school

Weber: One of Claire's best friends, Weber is a frog of few words.

Name ________________________________ Date ______________

Making Friends

Write About It: What do you think of the way Claire and her new friends are acting? How do you think Claire feels in this situation, and why? (Claire is the girl with the ponytail.) If you were Claire, what would you do next?

____

____

____

____

____

____

____

____

____

____

____

Keep Going: There is a saying that "New friends are silver; old friends are gold." What do you think this means? Do you agree? Write a letter to a dear friend you have not spoken to in a while. Tell your friend what he or she means to you.

Name ______________________ Date ____________

Top Secret

Write About It: What happens in the second half of the comic strip to make Claire want to read Amy's diary? Do you think it is ever okay to read another person's diary? Explain. Then predict what will happen next in the strip. Will Amy find out that Claire read her diary? Or will Claire admit what she has done? Write a paragraph telling what you think will happen.

____

____

____

____

____

____

____

____

Keep Going: Try keeping a diary for one week—pretending you are your favorite comic-strip character! Before you begin, brainstorm how your character talks and what kinds of things he or she thinks about.

Name ______________________________ Date ______________

Finders, Keepers

Write About It: Claire just discovered that the valuable trading card she found belongs to the not-so-nice class bully, Jason Grimes. Should Claire return the card to Jason—or keep it for herself? Why? Tell about a time you lost or found something valuable. How did you feel about the "finders keepers, losers weepers" rule?

____

____

____

____

____

____

____

____

____

____

Keep Going: Many schools don't let kids bring valuables such as trading cards on to school property. They worry that the toys will cause fights and other problems. What do you think: Should kids be allowed to bring valuable items to school? Why or why not?

Name ____________________ Date __________

Winning Votes

Write About It: What message is the cartoonist trying to get across with this comic strip? Before you answer, think about how Claire feels in the first three frames of the strip. Then think about how she must feel in the last frame. If you were Claire, would you vote for Raina in the school election? Why or why not? If you were voting in a school election, how would you decide whom to vote for?

____

____

____

____

____

____

____

____

____

Keep Going: If you were running for president of your class, what would you say and do to encourage students to vote for you? Write a speech that you would deliver to your classmates to earn their votes.

Name ______________________ Date ______________

Making the Grade

Write About It: What is Amy's attitude toward grades? If you were Amy's friend, what would you say to her? What is your own attitude toward grades? Do you get upset when you don't get the grade you had hoped for?

Keep Going: Some schools do not give grades at all. Instead, teachers write paragraphs explaining how each student is doing in each subject. What do you think about this method? Create a chart listing the pros and cons of a no-grading system.

Name ______________________________ Date ______________

On Schedule

Write About It: Based on the comic strip, how do you think Amy spends most of her time? (Amy is the girl with dark hair.) How do you think Claire likes to spend her time? What does Claire's comment in the last frame mean? Do you agree with her viewpoint? Why or why not?

____

____

____

____

____

____

____

____

____

____

Keep Going: If someone asked you to choose just one after-school activity, which one would you select? Why is this activity so interesting or important to you?

Name ______________________ Date ____________

Name Brands

GIGGLE
WHAT'S SO FUNNY, GIRL?
YOUR UNDERWEAR IS SHOWING, JASON GRIMES!
SO?!
—AND HOW ELSE ARE YOU GOING TO SEE THE LABEL?!!
12/8

Write About It: Why do you suppose Jason wants people to see the label on his underwear? Are you—or is anyone you know—very concerned about having clothes with the "right" designer labels? Why or why not?

____

____

____

____

____

____

____

____

____

____

Keep Going: What is more important to you when it comes to clothes: style or comfort? If you could design your own clothes, what would they look like? Would they have any unusual or interesting features? Would they have special pockets for certain belongings? Would they be self-cleaning? Use your imagination!

CITIZEN DOG

Created by Mark O'Hare

Background Information

Although *Citizen Dog* has only been on the comic-strip scene since 1995, it already enjoys tremendous popularity. The strip, which appears in more than 100 newspapers, focuses on the daily antics of a wisecracking dog named Fergus and his owner, Mel. Through the duo's conversations and experiences, cartoonist Mark O'Hare highlights the joys and pitfalls of everyday life, from ice cream cones to computer crashes.

Mark O'Hare has created newspaper comic strips since his college days in the late 1980s, but *Citizen Dog* is his first nationally syndicated strip. O'Hare's inspiration for Fergus the dog came entirely from his imagination; in fact, he does not even own a dog. O'Hare is also a talented animator and has worked as a storyboard artist for several animated television programs.

Cast of Characters

Fergus: A quick-witted dog who can speak, write, and outsmart his master

Mel: Fergus's owner, Mel does not always have the best of luck.

Maggie: One of Fergus's human friends

Cuddles: A neighborhood cat who witnesses many of Fergus's antics

Name ______________________ Date ____________

Eye on the Future

Write About It: What do you think of Fergus's prediction that electronic books will replace books made of paper? Do you believe this will happen? If so, how old do you think you will be when paper books become "extinct"? Would you enjoy reading books on computer, or would you miss the old-fashioned kind? Explain.

____

____

____

____

____

____

____

____

____

____

Keep Going: What else do you think will change in the next century? Make your own predictions for the future. What will homes look like? What activities will kids enjoy? How will people travel around? Provide plenty of details!

Name ______________________ Date ____________

Autumn Antics

Write About It: Do you think Maggie and Fergus like autumn? Why or why not? What is the fall like where you live? Describe the colors, smells in the air, weather, and anything else you can think of. What are some autumn activities that you enjoy?

Keep Going: What is your favorite season and why? Write a haiku about it. (A haiku is a three-line poem. The first and last lines each have five syllables, and the second line has seven syllables.)

Name ______________________ Date ____________

Dear Dog

Write About It: Write two letters: one that Fergus the dog might write to the president's dog and one that the president's dog might write back to Fergus. What would the two canines say to each other? What questions might Fergus ask about being a presidential pet? How might the dog respond? Use your imagination!

____

____

____

____

____

____

____

____

____

Keep Going: Which member of the First Family would you like to write to? Why? What would you say in your letter? Write a draft of your letter and send it to: The White House, 1600 Pennsylvania Ave., Washington, DC 20502. If you are writing to the president, you can go to www.whitehouse.gov to e-mail your message.

Name ______________________ Date ____________

A Dog's Day

Write About It: What—besides food—might Fergus write about in his diary? Pretend you are Fergus and record one day's thoughts and activities in a diary entry. Then decide if you agree with the conclusion Fergus reaches in the last frame of the comic strip? Why or why not?

____

____

____

____

____

____

____

____

____

____

Keep Going: Would you agree to spend one day as a dog? If so, what type of dog would you like to be and whom would you choose as your owner? If not, which other animal would you like to be for one day? Why? What do you think it would be like?

Name ________________________ Date ____________

Attention, Shoppers

Write About It: In this comic strip, Mel points out that people can do their grocery shopping on the Internet. Do you think the Internet will ever completely replace food stores or other types of stores (clothing, toys, and so on)? Why or why not? Do you agree with Fergus that shopping by computer "wouldn't be the same"? Explain.

Keep Going: There are Web sites for just about everything: stores, banks, airlines, and information of all kinds. If you were going to create a Web site, what would it be about? What kind of information could people find on it? What would it look like?

NANCY

Created by Guy and Brad Gilchrist

Background Information

Cartoonist Ernie Bushmiller created the comic character *Nancy* in the 1930s. Bushmiller's popular strip revolved around seven-year-old Nancy and her glamorous Aunt Fritzi. The cartoonist never explained to readers what happened to Nancy's mother and father, or why the little girl lived with her aunt, but readers did not seem to mind. The strip remained a mainstay of the funny pages for nearly five decades.

After Bushmiller's death in 1982, a cartoonist named Jerry Scott took over the comic. Although Scott's style was very different from Bushmiller's, the strip survived. In 1995, United Feature Syndicate decided to return the strip to its original look and hired comic artists Guy and Brad Gilchrist to revive Bushmiller's old-fashioned style. The brothers have been quite successful, and *Nancy* continues to attract readers young and old alike.

Cast of Characters

Nancy: A funny, often mischievous little girl with a wild imagination

Aunt Fritzi: Nancy's aunt and guardian

Sluggo: Nancy's best friend

Name ______________________ Date __________

Just Rewards?

Write About It: How does Nancy feel in the last part of this comic strip? Why do you think she feels that way? If you had studied all week for a test, how would you feel if it were canceled? What are some ways that you prepare for a test or quiz? Make a list and then share it with a partner.

____

____

____

____

____

____

____

____

____

Keep Going: Do you sometimes worry about how you will do on a big test? Make a list of five ways to beat test stress and stay calm. For example, do you feel more calm when you get a good night's rest the night before? When you are finished with your list, combine your tips with those of your classmates. Display the tips in your classroom.

Name ______________________________ Date ______________

In Your Dreams

NANCY reprinted by permission of United Feature Syndicate, Inc.

Write About It: What has Nancy done to remember her "cool" dreams? Choose one of Nancy's dreams and turn it into the plot for a new movie. Write a short summary telling what happens in the movie. (Don't forget to include a beginning, middle, and end.) Then list the actors and actresses you would choose to star in the movie.

____

____

____

____

____

____

____

____

____

____

Keep Going: Do you believe dreams are meaningful? Explain. Did you ever have a dream that related to events going on in your life?

Name ______________________ Date ____________

Four-Legged Forecast

Write About It: Who are the two "meteorological sources" (or weather experts) Nancy is talking about? How do you know? Does your pet (or a friend's pet) act strangely when a big storm is approaching? What does the animal do? How do *you* feel about stormy weather?

____

____

____

____

____

____

____

____

____

____

Keep Going: What do you suppose Nancy's pets are thinking or feeling in the comic strip? Imagine that the two animals can speak, and write the conversation they might be having.

Name ______________________ Date ____________

Stuck Inside

NANCY reprinted by permission of United Feature Syndicate, Inc.

Write About It: Why is Sluggo bothered by the rain? Do you ever feel this way? What is your favorite thing to do when you have outdoor recess? If you can't go outside because of the weather, how do you like to spend recess time?

Keep Going: In the comic, NODR stands for "No Out Door Recess." This is called an acronym. Another example of a weather acronym is SMILE, short for "Sunshine Means I Love Everyone!" Now create your own acronym to show how you feel about the weather. It can be as long or as short as you like.

Name ____________________ Date __________

Pooch Party

Write About It: Were you surprised by the ending of this comic strip? Why or why not? Have you ever heard of anyone throwing a birthday party for a dog or other pet? What do you think of the idea? Describe other ways Nancy, Aunt Fritzi, and Poochie might celebrate at the party. What other foods might they eat? What games might they play?

Keep Going: Choose a pet you know (it could be yours, a friend's or neighbor's, or even a cartoon pet). If this animal could write a birthday wish list, what would it ask for? (The animal might prefer a gift that is not an object, such as a whole day playing in the park.) Imagine that you are the pet, and make a descriptive list of its birthday wishes.

ADDITIONAL RESOURCES

If your students want to know more about a particular comic strip or cartoonist, or if you would like to read additional comics, consult the following Web sites and books. These resources will help you make comic strips a regular part of your creative-writing repertoire.

Web Sites

http://www.uexpress.com Visit this Universal Press Syndicate site for archives of *Citizen Dog*, *Garfield*, and dozens of other nationally syndicated strips.

http://www.unitedmedia.com/comics Fans will find plenty of *Peanuts*, *Nancy*, and other strips at this United Media site.

http://www.kingfeatures.com The home page for King Features Syndicate includes samples and information on *Dennis the Menace*, *Claire and Weber*, and many other strips.

http://www.garfield.com This official *Garfield* site includes interviews with creator Jim Davis, news about the strip, games, and an online catalog.

Books for the Teacher

The World Encyclopedia of Comics edited by Maurice Horn (Chelsea House, 1998). This updated, comprehensive resource covers all aspects of comics from around the globe.

100 Years of American Newspaper Comics: An Illustrated Encyclopedia edited by Maurice Horn (Gramercy Books, 1996). This volume contains in-depth background on many popular comic strips.

Books for Children

Citizen Dog by Mark O'Hare (Andrews McMeel Publishing, 1998). This is a hilarious collection of *Citizen Dog* strips.

Dennis the Menace: His First 40 Years by Hank Ketcham (Abbeville Press, 1991). This is an amusing anthology of classic *Dennis* comics.

Funny Papers: Behind the Scenes of Comics by Elaine Scott (William Morrow & Co., 1993). This book includes a brief history of comics plus a fascinating look at how comics are created, sold, printed, and distributed.

Garfield Goes to Waist by Jim Davis (Paws, Inc., 1990). Check your local library and bookstore for this and other rollicking collections of *Garfield* strips.

The World Is Filled With Mondays by Charles M. Schulz (Harper, 1999). Check your local library or bookstore for this and other paperback collections of beloved *Peanuts* strips.

TOPICAL INDEX

Use this index to locate a comic strip or prompt related to a particular topic.